PALM BEACH COUNTY
LIBRARY SYSTEM

3650 Summit Boulevard
West Palm Beach, FL 33406

CUBAN IMMIGRANTS
IN THEIR SHOES

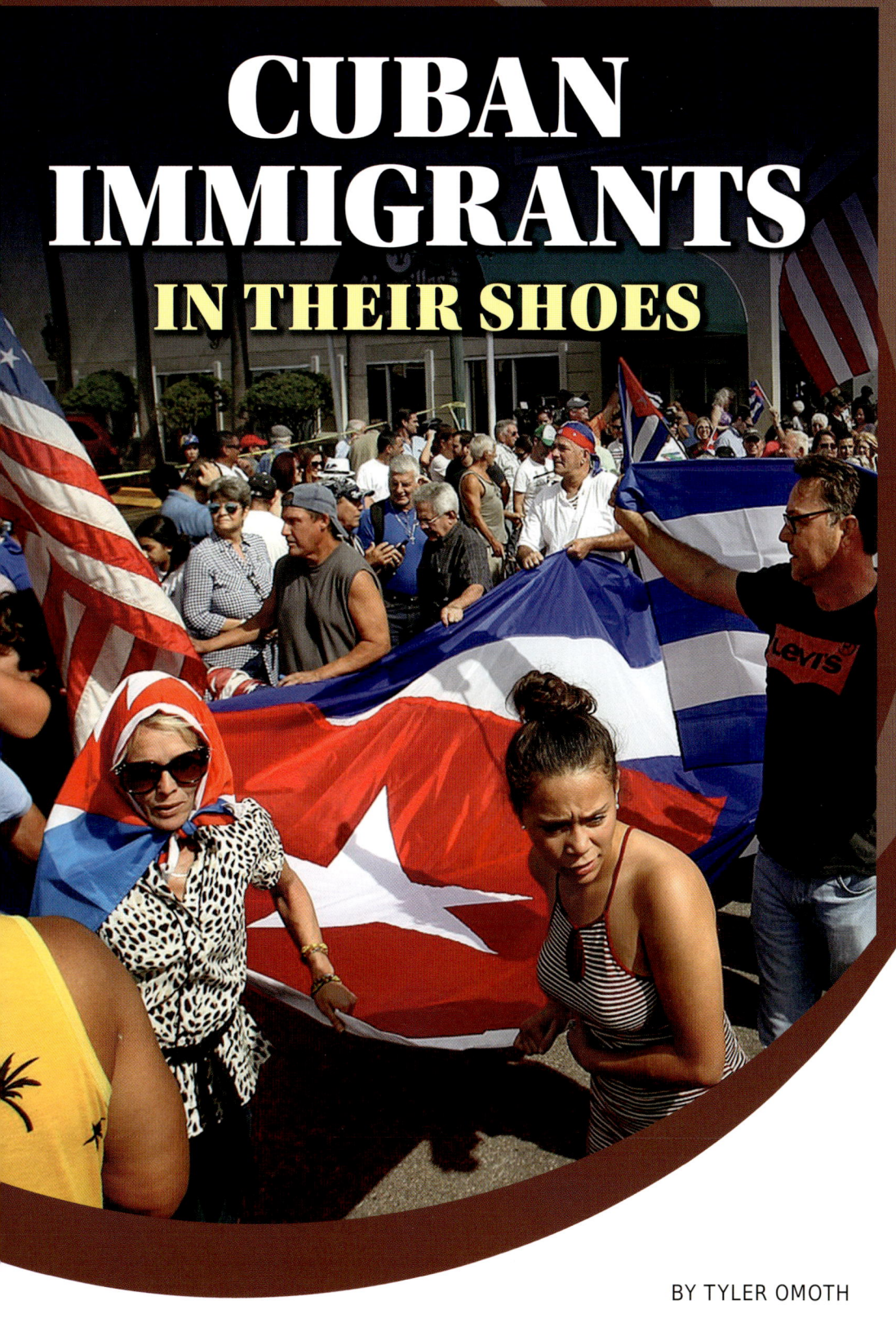

BY TYLER OMOTH

Published by The Child's World®
1980 Lookout Drive • Mankato, MN 56003-1705
800-599-READ • www.childsworld.com

Content Consultant: Aviva Chomsky, Professor of History and Coordinator of Latin American Studies, Salem State University

Photographs ©: Marsha Halper/Miami Herald/AP Images, cover, 1; Andrew St. George/AP Images, 6; AP Images, 9, 10; Everett Historical/Shutterstock Images, 12; Lorraine Boogich/iStockphoto, 15; Shutterstock Images, 16; Kobby Dagan/Shutterstock Images, 18; Red Line Editorial, 20; Bill Cooke/AP Images, 21; C. M. Guerrero/El Nuevo Herald/AP Images, 22; Patrick Farrell/KRT/Newscom, 24; Liz Balmaseda/MCT/Newscom, 27; David Adame/AP Images, 28

Copyright © 2018 by The Child's World®
All rights reserved. No part of this book may be reproduced or utilized in any form or by any means without written permission from the publisher.

ISBN 9781503820258
LCCN 2016960925

Printed in the United States of America
PA02338

ABOUT THE AUTHOR

Tyler Omoth has written more than 30 books for kids on many different topics. He loves sports (especially baseball), animals, and beaches. He lives in sunny Brandon, Florida, with his wife, Mary, and their very demanding cat, Josie.

TABLE OF CONTENTS

Fast Facts and Timeline 4

Chapter 1
Leaving Cuba 6

Chapter 2
Swimming toward Freedom 12

Chapter 3
Dancing with Joy 18

Chapter 4
The Language of Music 24

Think About It 29
Glossary 30
Source Notes 31
To Learn More 32
Index 32

FAST FACTS

Important Numbers

- Approximately 124,000 Cuban Americans were in the United States at the beginning of 1959.
- In 2013, approximately 1,144,000 Cuban Americans were first-generation immigrants, meaning they were born in Cuba.
- Nearly 2 million Cuban Americans were in the United States as of 2016.

Where Cuban Immigrants Settled

- Miami, Florida
- New York, New York
- Tampa, Florida
- Long Beach, California

Reasons for Immigrating

- Some immigrants feared the Cuban government.
- Many Cubans suffered from poverty and unemployment.
- Cubans moved to the United States hoping to find safety and new opportunities to earn a living.

TIMELINE

- **1959:** The Cuban **Revolution** is victorious, with Fidel Castro and a new revolutionary government coming to power.
- **1959:** The first major wave of Cuban immigration to the United States begins.
- **1959:** The first Coast Guard boat rescue of Cuban immigrants occurs.
- **1961:** U.S. president John F. Kennedy ends **diplomatic ties** with Cuba.
- **1965:** Castro opens the port of Camarioca for Cubans wishing to leave.
- **1965:** The second major wave of Cuban migration to the United States begins.
- **1980:** Castro opens the port of Mariel for those wishing to leave. This leads to the third major wave of Cuban migration to the United States.
- **1993:** Following the 1991 collapse of the Soviet Union, the fourth major wave of Cuban migration to the United States begins.
- **2014:** The United States and Cuba begin to restore diplomatic ties.

Chapter 1

LEAVING CUBA

María de los Angeles Torres touched the thick glass. On the other side of the divider, her parents smiled weakly and waved. María clutched her doll. She tried not to cry.

All around her, other Cuban children said tearful good-byes to their parents. María did not know their stories. She did not know anyone on this side of the glass. They were like fish in a *pecera*, or fishbowl.

◀ **Fidel Castro led a group of rebels that took over Cuba in 1959.**

Six-year-old María was waiting to board a plane in Havana, Cuba. It was July 30, 1961. María and many other children were about to take a flight to Miami, Florida. Officials were inspecting the children's luggage and documents. Then the children would leave their homeland.

María had never been out of Cuba before. But she understood why her parents wanted her to leave the country. A few months earlier, in April, Cuban officials had warned that the United States was invading Cuba. María remembered curling up in a bathtub next to her sister. Her parents had told them the bathtub was the safest place in the house. María didn't get any sleep that night. Gunfire and the hum of overhead planes kept her awake. In the end, nothing happened to their house. The U.S. invasion had failed. However, María's parents feared that a second U.S. attack would follow.

María's parents also feared Cuba's leader, Fidel Castro. They had supported Castro when he overthrew **dictator** Fulgencio Batista in 1959. But Castro did not turn out to be the fair leader María's parents hoped he would be. Castro jailed or killed people who opposed him.

Castro's government also closed many private schools. María's parents heard rumors that Castro would open new schools. The schools would teach children to support Castro.

María's parents acted quickly. They had heard about Operation Pedro Pan (1960–1962). It was a rescue program that the U.S. government had set up. The program flew children from Havana to Miami. Now María would be one of thousands of Cuban children flown to the United States.

Officials gave back María's suitcase and handbag. She followed the rest of the children onto the runway. She turned to look at her parents one last time. They had promised to follow her to the United States later, along with her three younger sisters. Operation Pedro Pan flew children 6 to 16 years old. Her sisters were too young for the program.

On the plane, María touched the name tag on her dress. She reread the phone number on the tag.

> "Not having your parents there, you kind of feel a sense of betrayal, that you're betraying your parents if you're too happy. . . . You feel this sense that you should never or can never be really happy."
> —Carlos Eire, who was one of the Pedro Pan children[1]

▲ **Passengers arrive in Miami after the short flight from Cuba in 1961.**

It belonged to the Greers, her parents' friends in Miami. María would be staying with them. She did not know the couple well. But it would only be for a short time, she thought.

After a 45-minute plane ride, María arrived in Miami. At the time, many people in Miami were not friendly to Cubans. María later remembered it as the place "where you knelt down, thanked the United States for bringing you, and at the same time apologized for being Cuban."[2]

María noticed **racism** everywhere. It was difficult for many Cubans to find housing. María saw For Rent signs that read "No Children, No Pets, No Cubans."[3] She heard stories about Cubans who had a hard time finding jobs.

María herself knew little English. She had enjoyed school in Cuba. But in Miami, she had a hard time understanding what the teachers were saying. The Greers were nice to her. But she had never lived apart from her family.

The Greers helped María obtain **visa** waivers. These documents would allow María's family to travel to the United States. Her family arrived in Miami four months later. María had been lucky. Many Pedro Pan children did not see their families for many years. Some never saw their parents again.

As an adult, María studied Operation Pedro Pan. She interviewed other Pedro Pan children. She revisited Cuba. It was not the same Cuba of her childhood, before Castro's revolution. But she would always cherish the good memories she had of Cuba. "I want to keep looking at the relationships and complexities of Cubans here (in the United States) and there (in Cuba)," she said. "My life is very much here, but I can't forget where I came from."[4]

◀ **Cuban immigrants gather in Miami in 1961, preparing to fight against Fidel Castro in Cuba.**

Chapter 2

SWIMMING TOWARD FREEDOM

Jose Auraz stepped into the ocean and began swimming. The 29-year-old swam at least 4 miles (6.4 km) every day. He practiced in Guantanamo Bay near his hometown of Caimanera, Cuba. When people asked him why he was training so hard, he told them he was training for a big competition.

"When I go (to) Havana, I want first place," he said.[5]

◀ **The United States has had a military base in Guantanamo Bay since 1903.**

But there was no swimming competition in Havana. Auraz was training for a much bigger prize. He was planning to swim to U.S.–controlled waters in Guantanamo Bay.

Guantanamo Bay lies along the southeast coast of Cuba. The United States controls the part of the bay south of Caimanera. Auraz knew he would be safe if he could swim to this part of the bay. He would be in U.S. territory.

The year was 1993. The Soviet Union, Cuba's once-powerful ally, had collapsed two years earlier. Cuba's economy had collapsed with it. Thousands of workers lost their jobs. And a food shortage was causing many Cubans to go hungry.

Auraz had a job with the Cuban military. But he and many others struggled to make a living. Auraz wanted a better life for himself. He no longer wanted to live under a **Communist** government.

One night, Auraz slipped away from a birthday party and walked down to the coast. The beach was dark, and he could hear rain starting to hit the water. He wore his military uniform. The patrol officers mistook him for another officer.

Auraz retreated to some bushes when no one was looking. He changed into swim trunks. Then he covered his body in motor oil.

13

Fishermen had told him the oil would keep sharks away. Auraz looked back at the party. Then he took a deep breath and jumped into the water.

He swam steadily for more than an hour. Suddenly, a light shone in his eyes. He heard U.S. soldiers shouting from their boat. The U.S. military, thinking Auraz might be a spy, kept him locked up for nine days. But eventually, they let him go. They dropped him off in Miami. U.S. immigration policy stated that any Cuban found in U.S. waters must be allowed to stay in the United States.

Auraz was all alone. "I had no ID with me . . . no sleeping bag. No blanket," he later said.[6] Even though Auraz had very little, he was thrilled. He had made it to the United States.

But life was harder than he had expected. Many Cuban immigrants lived in Florida, and there were not enough jobs. Auraz walked the streets of Miami, asking business after business if they would let him work. Eventually, he found a job washing dishes.

At the end of his first day, his hands were tired, wrinkled, and worn. Auraz then went to a shelter. He lay on a bare cot next to dozens of other people he didn't know. It was a tough life, but it was a start.

▶ Many Cuban immigrants live in a Miami neighborhood known as Little Havana.

Without **work papers**, Auraz struggled to find good jobs. He decided to leave Miami and move west. He worked in low-paying labor jobs wherever he went. He married in Nevada, but his wife later died from cancer. He moved to California and remarried. He had two children, but he and his wife divorced. Homeless and depressed, Auraz traveled to Montana. A shelter took him in. Surrounded by the beautiful Rocky Mountains, he started feeling hopeful again. He found another job washing dishes.

Auraz needed a lawyer to apply for permanent residency. Unfortunately, he couldn't afford to hire one. But a woman who worked at the shelter heard about his case. She found a lawyer who would help him for free.

Finally, on July 28, 2009, Auraz received his permanent resident identification card. At last, he had proof that he was a legal resident of the United States. "My life changed when I received my employment authorization," he said.[7]

Auraz began working to help other immigrants who were struggling. Though his sights were set on a future in the United States, he missed his family back home. He had chosen to leave Cuba. But he would never forget what he had left behind.

◀ **Immigrants without work papers often have to take jobs that do not pay well, such as washing dishes.**

Chapter 3

DANCING WITH JOY

Neri Torres waited for the perfect moment. The year was 1990, and she was traveling in Italy with a group of Cuban dancers. But Torres had a secret. She planned to sneak away to start a new life. Unfortunately, the escape did not go according to plan. Someone discovered her secret, and she had to go back to Cuba.

◀ **Cuba is known for a style of dance known as rumba.**

Torres had tried to leave Cuba before. Ten years earlier, her family had scattered onto several boats, rushing through the rough seas toward the United States. Her older sister and brother had made it. But the boat Torres was on was taken back to the shores of Cuba.

Torres knew she needed to get out of Cuba if she was going to have the life she dreamed of. "I used to sit and hang out on the sea wall and think about what's beyond the sea," she later said. "I love my people. I love my family. But I feel trapped. That's the sensation you have when you live in Cuba."[8]

Torres had known from a young age that she loved to dance. She followed her dream and began to study ballet when she was 12 years old. She continued studying dance as an adult, and she dreamed of dancing in the United States.

But after her failed attempt to flee in 1990, Torres wondered if she would ever make it. The next year, she travelled to Italy once again to dance. This time, she successfully separated herself from the group. After that, she made her way to Miami.

But she was alone in her new country. "Being an immigrant is not an easy ride in the park," Torres said. "You are leaving all your roots . . . your background . . . even your way of eating."[9]

Torres thought about her family members who were still back in Cuba. She also wondered where in the United States she might find her brother and sister.

Like many Cubans, Torres had African **heritage**. In Miami, she found many people like her. This inspired her to keep dancing in the ways she knew best. Even so, she struggled to find work.

CUBAN IMMIGRATION TO THE UNITED STATES

Years	Number of immigrants
1920-1929	12,769
1930-1939	10,641
1940-1949	25,976
1950-1959	73,221
1960-1969	202,030
1970-1979	256,497
1980-1989	132,552
1990-1999	159,037
2000-2009	271,742
2010-2014	180,032

▲ **Gloria Estefan, a Cuban immigrant, became a popular singer in the 1980s and 1990s.**

"I didn't have any experience as a cashier. . . . But I kept dancing no matter what," she said.[10]

It didn't take long for people in the United States to take notice. In just a few years, Torres had become a successful dancer in the United States. She started dancing with Gloria Estefan and the Miami Sound Machine, a popular music group. Soon, Torres was also helping to create dance scenes in movies.

But Torres was not done. In 1999, she watched dancers impress a huge crowd with a routine she had created. It was the Super Bowl pregame show. This was one of the biggest stages in the world. Torres saw the camera flashes and heard the roar of the crowd. This was her dream come true.

While she continued her career, Torres started a dancing studio in Miami. She taught traditional Afro-Cuban dances to other immigrants. The studio helped set up festivals and classes all around the Miami area. Torres was delighted that Afro-Cuban immigrants were discovering their heritage through the language of dance.

For Torres, being a Cuban immigrant in the United States meant she had the best of both worlds. She embraced the **culture** of her roots while enjoying the life she had yearned for as a child.

◀ **Cuban American ballet dancers practice in a Miami studio.**

Chapter 4

THE LANGUAGE OF MUSIC

Twelve-year-old Lizbet Martinez was sitting at home with her father. He had a serious look on his face. "Do you want to leave?" he asked her.[11] Lizbet said yes.

The year was 1994. The government of Cuba had recently made an announcement. Anyone who wanted to leave the country would not be stopped.

◀ **Thousands of Cubans have risked their lives to reach the United States.**

Cubans were leaving by the thousands in boats and homemade rafts. They hoped to make it to the United States. Very few children had a choice, but Lizbet did. She said yes because she knew her family had always wanted to leave.

A few nights later, the family boarded a rickety raft. Lizbet had only a small bag with a few clothes in it. She also had her most prized possession, a violin. She had studied the instrument for years and was now very good at playing it.

Lizbet and her family bounced around on the ocean for several days. Waves threatened to overturn the small raft. No one knew if sharks or other predators were in the water around them. Nights were especially scary because of the darkness.

One morning around four o'clock, the U.S. Coast Guard spotted them. The U.S. sailors approached the raft. They began bringing the Cuban immigrants onto their much larger boat.

> "Once you're alone in the ocean and can't see Cuba or anything else to the north, that's when you start praying, asking God, 'What's going to happen with my life?'"
>
> —Lizbet Martinez[12]

25

But as the sailors helped people aboard, they tossed away all of their belongings. Lizbet couldn't bear the thought of them throwing away her violin.

"They did not know Spanish, and we did not speak English, but I figured they would know the American national anthem," she said. "So that's when I got my violin and began to play it."[13]

It worked. The sailors were impressed with her courage and her violin skills. They let her keep the instrument. Lizbet and her family were held at Guantanamo Bay, an area where Cuban **refugees** waited for identification and passage to the United States. While waiting there, Lizbet continued to play.

News cameras from around the world were in Guantanamo Bay. Reporters were covering the Cuban rafter crisis. Many Cubans were dying in their attempts to get to the United States. But when the cameras and microphones found Lizbet playing her violin, she became famous instantly.

Lizbet and her family made it to the United States. And she quickly realized that people recognized her and her violin. She was even asked to play "The Star-Spangled Banner" for U.S. president Bill Clinton.

The 12-year-old girl still knew very little English. But each time she played, she said a few words, pleading for her people. "Thank you for all," she said. "Please open your hearts."[14]

When Lizbet grew up, she became a teacher in Miami. For much of her career, she taught music. She kept the violin that had come with her on the raft, but she stopped playing it. She bought a new violin, which she started playing for church gatherings and friends.

▲ **Lizbet plays her violin for a group of refugees.**

▲ **Lizbet gives a violin lesson to a student in 2003.**

Looking back 20 years later, Lizbet had no regrets. "I am very grateful to my parents, who left their own parents behind so that I could live in freedom," she said.[15]

Today, Cubans have become a large part of U.S. culture. This is especially true in South Florida, where many Cuban immigrants have settled. Cuban restaurants, music, and style have added to the diversity of cultures in the area.

Many Cubans have risked their lives to immigrate to the United States. However, not all have achieved the success they dreamed of. Life continues to be a challenge for large numbers of Cuban immigrants. They struggle with unemployment and low wages. But for many, the risk was worth the reward. Some Cuban Americans are successful teachers, business owners, and politicians. They embrace their Cuban heritage while striving for a better life in the United States.

THINK ABOUT IT

- Why do you think many immigrants were willing to leave part of their family in Cuba when they moved to the United States? What would you have done if you were in their situation?
- Imagine you had to leave your home to start a new life somewhere else, and you could bring only one personal item. What would you bring? Why?
- What do you think it would it be like to be sent to a new country, all by yourself, where you didn't know the language?

GLOSSARY

Communist (KAHM-yoo-nist): Communist means having to do with a system in which the government controls the economy. Many Cubans left the country to escape its Communist government.

culture (KUL-chur): Culture is the ideas and way of life that define a group of people. Cuban culture involves dance, music, food, sports, and more.

dictator (DIK-tay-tur): A dictator is a person who rules a country, often in a way that is harsh or cruel. Many considered Fidel Castro, who led Cuba's government until 2006, a dictator.

diplomatic ties (dip-luh-MAT-ik TYZ): Diplomatic ties are relationships between countries' governments. Cuba and the United States cut off diplomatic ties in the 1960s.

heritage (HER-i-tij): Heritage is a group's beliefs and traditions that shape their history and identity. Cuban immigrants start new lives in the United States, but many hold on to their heritage.

racism (RAY-sih-zum): Racism is a belief that people with certain skin colors or cultures are better than others. Some Cuban immigrants faced racism when they came to the United States.

refugees (ref-yoo-JEEZ): Refugees are people who seek safety in a foreign country, especially to avoid war or other dangers. Many refugees came to the United States to escape Cuba's government.

revolution (rev-uh-LOO-shun): A revolution is an event in which a group takes over a government. Fidel Castro led the Cuban Revolution in the late 1950s.

visa (VEE-zuh): A visa is a document or stamp that shows permission for a person to enter another country. The immigrant received a visa that allowed her to travel to the United States.

work papers (WURK PAY-purz): Work papers are documents that certify that an employee is able to legally work. Without working papers, it is hard for immigrants to find good jobs.

SOURCE NOTES

1. "Children of Cuba Remember Their Flight to America." *NPR*. NPR, 19 Nov. 2011. Web. 7 Dec. 2016.

2. Lisa Stodder. "Profile: María de los Angeles Torres." *UIC News*. The Board of Trustees of the University of Illinois, 8 Mar. 2006. Web. 7 Dec. 2016.

3. María de los Angeles Torres. *In the Land of Mirrors: Cuban Exile Politics in the United States*. Ann Arbor, MI: University of Michigan Press, 1999. Print. 73.

4. Nancy Traver. "Memories of Cuba Inspire Book by DePaul Professor." *Temple University*. Temple University, 4 June 2003. Web. 7 Dec. 2016.

5. Kiela Szpaller. "American Story: Cuban Refugee Overcame 82-Minute Swim, Family Tragedies, Addictions to Make New Life in U.S., Montana." *Missoulian*. Missoulian, 15 Aug. 2009. Web. 7 Dec. 2016.

6. Ibid.

7. Ibid.

8. "The Voices." *Voices from Cuba*. Big Pictures International, n.d. Web. 7 Dec. 2016.

9. Barbara Corbellini Duarte. "Dance Festival Shares Stories of New Lives in Strange Places." *SouthFlorida.com*. South Florida, 19 Aug. 2015. Web. 7 Dec. 2016.

10. Neri Torres. Personal communication. 11 Oct. 2016.

11. Miami Herald. "Cuban Rafters: 20 Years after the Crisis — A Young Violinist Remembers." Online video. *YouTube*. YouTube, 30 Aug. 2014. Web. 7 Dec. 2016.

12. Ibid.

13. Nora Gámez Torres. "Young Cuban Rafter Who Played Star-Spangled Banner on Boat Is Now a Mom and Teacher in Hialeah." *Miami Herald*. Miami Herald, 31 Aug. 2014. Web. 7 Dec. 2016.

14. Hank Tester. "All Grown Up: The Face of the Cuban Rafter Crisis." *NBC Miami*. NBCUniversal Media, 23 Sept. 2010. Web. 7 Dec. 2016.

15. Miami Herald. "Cuban Rafters: 20 Years after the Crisis — A Young Violinist Remembers." Online video. *YouTube*. YouTube, 30 Aug. 2014. Web. 7 Dec. 2016.

TO LEARN MORE

Books

Conley, Kate. *Cuba*. Mankato, MN: The Child's World, 2016.

Edwards, Sue Bradford. *12 Incredible Facts about the Cuban Missile Crisis*. North Mankato, MN: 12-Story Library, 2016.

Gregory, Joy. *Cuba*. New York, NY: AV2 by Weigl, 2017.

Web Sites

Visit our Web site for links about Cuban immigrants: childsworld.com/links

Note to Parents, Teachers, and Librarians: We routinely verify our Web links to make sure they are safe and active sites. So encourage your readers to check them out!

INDEX

Auraz, Jose, 12–17

Batista, Fulgencio, 7

Caimanera, Cuba, 12–13

Castro, Fidel, 7–8, 11

Clinton, Bill, 26

Coast Guard, U.S., 25

Estefan, Gloria, 21

Guantanamo Bay, 12–13, 26

Havana, Cuba, 7–8, 12–13

Martinez, Lizbet, 24–28

Miami, Florida, 7–11, 14, 17, 19–23, 27

Operation Pedro Pan, 8, 11

racism, 11

Soviet Union, 13

Super Bowl, 23

Torres, María de los Angeles, 6–11

Torres, Neri, 18–23

32